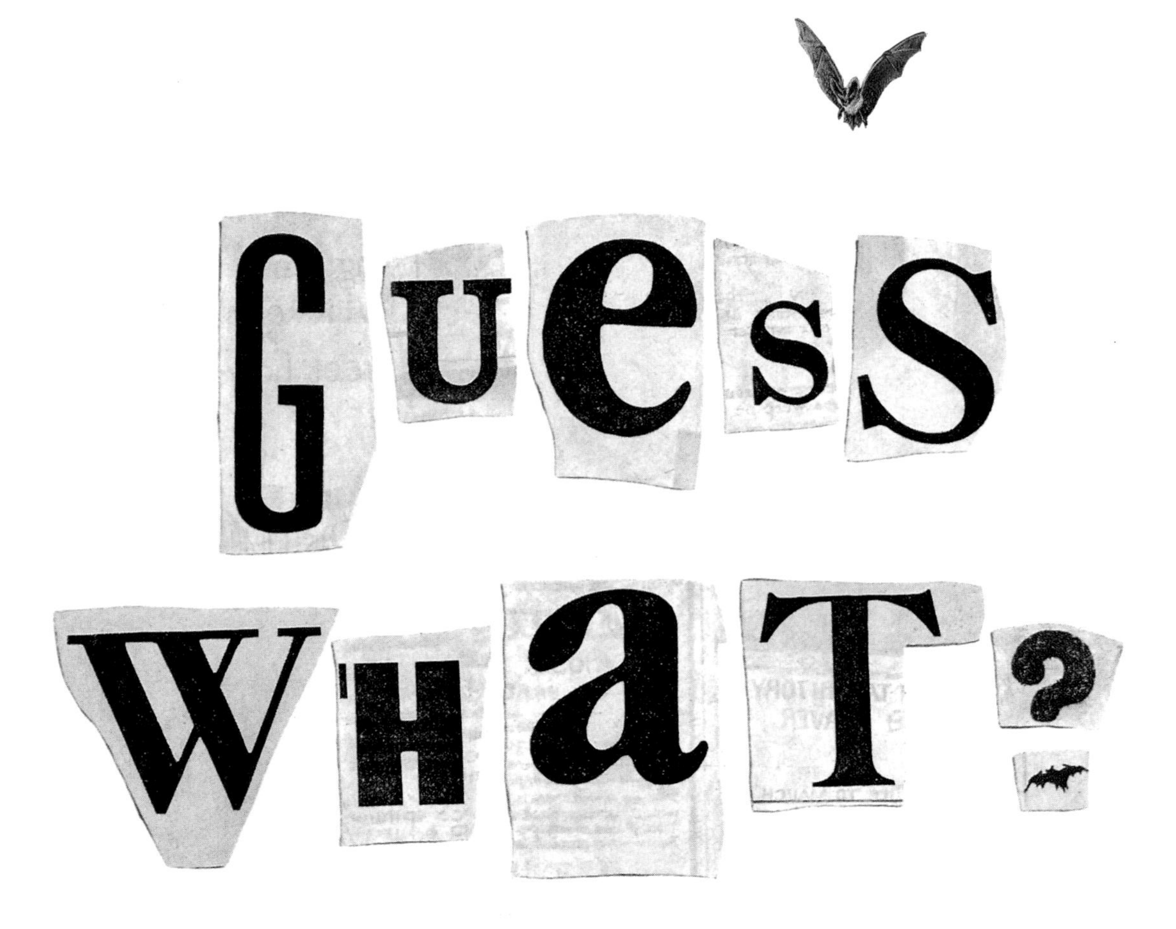

Written by Mem Fox

Illustrated by Vivienne Goodman

Gulliver Books
Harcourt Brace Jovanovich, Publishers
San Diego New York London

First published 1988 by Omnibus Books

Library of Congress Cataloging-in-Publication Data
Fox, Mem, 1946–
Guess what?/Mem Fox and Vivienne Goodman.
p. cm.
"Gulliver books."
Summary: Through a series of questions to which the reader must answer yes or no, the personality and occupation of a lady called Daisy O'Grady are revealed.
ISBN 0-15-200452-1
[1. Identify—Fiction. 2. Questions and answers—Fiction.]
I. Goodman, Vivienne, ill. II. Title.
PZ7.F8373Gu 1990
[E]—dc20 90-4127

The paintings in this book were executed in gouache on watercolor paper. The originals are the same size as the reproductions you see here.
The text type was set in Caxton Book by Central Graphics, San Diego, California.
Printed and bound by Tien Wah Press, Singapore
Production supervision by Warren Wallerstein and Ginger Boyer
Text design by Lydia D'moch

D E F

To Miss Nancy and Wilfrid Gordon
McDonald Partridge
—M. F.

To Tom and Sarah
—V. G.

Far away from here lives
a crazy lady called
Daisy O'Grady.

Is she tall?

Guess!

Is she thin?

Guess!

HORRID HAG!
OLD WITCH
SKIN AND BONES!
YES!
SKINNY OLD GIT!
THIN!
LIKE A TOOTHPICK
FROGGIES
IRISH LINEN
NEW FRESH FRAGRANCE
Velvet
Cold
Johnson's baby powder
375g NET

Yes!

Does she wear a long black dress?

Guess!

PEGS
CAN BE SUCH
BOARS

Yes!

Is she fond of animals?

Guess!

THE WEEKEND AUSTRALIAN
Language is a virus
APPY TOM

Yes!

Has she got a cat that's really sleek and black?

Guess!

Yes!

Does she sometimes wear a hat?

Guess!

I SCARE MYSELF
BEWARE OF THE BOG
ZAPPA
BIZARRE
THE doors
Ja!
WHICH?
VISIT NARNIA TODAY!
CHINA
Magazine 17
Profitable gardening for pleasure
The voice that tells you to find
second
$540 per month, now.
The meaning of it all
AMONG THE SWEEPING
BROOM STICKS
SEEMS to COME
FROM HIGH IN THE AIR

Is it as black as her dress and her cat?

Guess!

oui
WHO ARE YOU
HATFUL OF HOLLOW
HIROSHIMA NEVER AGAIN
DOGS BREATH
BAD
Idiot grin

Yes!

Does she like cooking?

Guess!

TASTY OLD TOE-NAILS
FOIL RECIPES
WITCHES CORNFLOUR
For delicious
Golden Crust
PLAIN
2kg NET
flour
with WEEVILS
HANDLE
ed toads
PLASMA
LIZARDS' LIVER PUREE
DEFENDER
PELLETS
KILLS NASTIES
WARNING
500gm

Yes!

Does she mix rats' tails, toenails,
and dead lizards' scales?

Guess!

Diploma
FREE Plastic Nasty Inside
IFELESS LIZARDS
SCALE POWDER
EEZE-DRIED LACE MONITOR, BLUE-TONGUE, GOANNA,
INK, THORNY DEVIL KNOB-TAILED GECKO, STUMPY-TAIL,
NIFEX SNAKE-LIZARD, LAKE EYRE DRAGON, TWO-TOED
SERT SKINK AND FRILLED NECK LIZARD SCALE MIX.
NET 500g
•LOW IN SUGAR
•LOW IN FAT
•HIGH IN PROTEIN
WITH MAGGOTS
LENNON
BRAND
SHAVED FISH
HEINZ
BLOOD S
Sunbeam
MIXMASTER
McCHUCK
Blowfly
Eyes
PORKSNOT & C
MUCUS
PICKLE
HAND-PICKE
TABASCO
Cadbury
BOURNVILLE
COCOA
KEEN'S
MUSTARD

Does she have a broomstick?

Guess!

NON TOCCATE
MAKE TEA NOT LOVE
KEEP OUT
OUI
OUI
BROOMHILDA WAS HERE
HANSEL + GRETEL TOO!
TOAD + RATTY 1731

Yes!

Does she like to fly at night?

Guess!

Yes!

Is she a cursing, cackling,
cranky old witch?

Guess!

SEX PISTOLS
HOT RATS
BAD
KISS ME
BLOW
FLIES
Idiot grin

Some people say she's really mean.

But guess what?